NOW YOU CAN READ.....
Little Red Riding Hood

STORY ADAPTED BY LUCY KINCAID

ILLUSTRATED BY ERIC ROWE

BRIMAX BOOKS • CAMBRIDGE • ENGLAND

Little Red Riding Hood's mother was packing a basket with eggs and butter and homemade bread.

"Who is that for?" asked Little Red Riding Hood.

"For Grandma," said Mother. "She has not been feeling well." Grandma lived alone in a cottage in the middle of the wood.

"I will take it to her," said Little Red Riding Hood. She put on her red cape with the red hood and picked up the basket.

"Make sure you go straight to the cottage," said Mother as she waved goodbye. "And do not talk to any strangers."

Little Red Riding Hood meant to go straight to the cottage but there were so many wild flowers growing in the wood, she decided to stop and pick some for Grandma. Grandma liked flowers. They would cheer her up.

"Good morning," said a voice at her elbow. It was a wolf. "Where are you taking these goodies?" he asked, peeping inside the basket.

"I am taking them to my Grandma," said Little Red Riding Hood, quite forgetting what her mother had said about talking to strangers. "Lucky Grandma," said the wolf. "Where does she live?"

"In the cottage in the middle of the wood," said Little Red Riding Hood.

"Be sure to pick her a nice BIG bunch of flowers," said the wolf, and hurried away.

The wolf went
straight to
Grandma's cottage.
He knocked at the
door.
"Who is there?"
called Grandma.
"It is I, Little
Red Riding Hood,"
replied the wolf
in a 'little girl'
voice.
"Then lift up the
latch and come in,"
called Grandma.

Grandma screamed loudly when she saw the wolf's face peering round the door. He was licking his lips. She jumped out of bed and into the cupboard, and locked herself in.

The wolf picked up her frilly bed-cap, which had fallen to the floor, and put it on his own head. He pushed his ears inside the cap then climbed into Grandma's bed. He pulled the covers up round his neck, then sat and waited for Little Red Riding Hood to come.

Presently, there was a knock at the door.

"Who is there?" he called, in a voice that sounded like Grandma's.

"It is I, Little Red Riding Hood," replied Little Red Riding Hood.

"Then lift up the latch and come in," called the sly, old wolf.

Little Red Riding Hood lifted the latch and went in. "Are you feeling better, Grandma?" she asked.

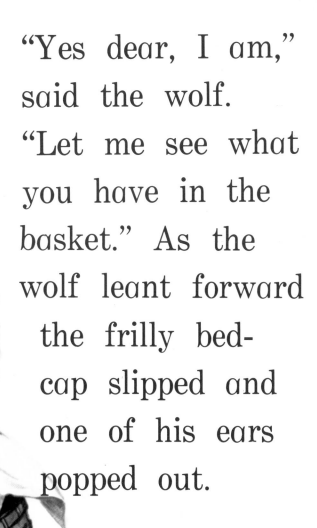

"Yes dear, I am," said the wolf. "Let me see what you have in the basket." As the wolf leant forward the frilly bed-cap slipped and one of his ears popped out.

"What big ears you have," said Little Red Riding Hood.
"All the better to hear you with my dear," said the wolf, turning towards her.

"What big eyes you have," said Little Red Riding Hood, beginning to feel just a tiny bit frightened. "All the better to see you with," said the wolf, with a big grin.

"What big teeth you have," said Little Red Riding Hood, now feeling very frightened indeed.

"All the better to EAT you with," said the wolf and he threw back the covers and jumped out of bed.

"You are not my Grandma!"
screamed Little Red Riding Hood.

"No, I am not. I am the big bad
wolf," growled the wolf in his own
voice. "And I am going to eat
you up."

"Help! Help!" screamed Little Red Riding Hood as the wolf chased her out of the cottage and into the wood.

The woodcutter heard her screams
and came to the rescue. As soon
as the wolf saw the woodcutter's
big wood-cutting axe, he put his
tail between his legs and ran
away as fast as he could.

Little Red Riding Hood told the woodcutter what had happened. "Where is your Grandma now?" asked the woodcutter.

"I do not know," sobbed Little Red Riding Hood. "Perhaps that horrid wolf has eaten her."

But when they got back to the cottage, they heard the sound of knocking coming from inside the cupboard and a voice asking if it was safe to come out.

"It is me Grandma!" called Little Red Riding Hood.

Only when Grandma was REALLY sure, did she unlock the cupboard door.

"What a lucky escape we have both had," said Little Red Riding Hood as she hugged Grandma.

What a lucky escape indeed.

All these appear in the pages of the story. Can you find them?

Mother

Little Red Riding Hood

Grandma

flowers